WILLIAM AND
THE WOLVES

By the same author

Henry Hobbs, Alien
Poor Little Mary

Kathryn Cave

WILLIAM AND THE WOLVES

Illustrated by Stephen Player

For Alice

VIKING

Published by the Penguin Group
Penguin Books Ltd, 27 Wrights Lane, London W8 5TZ, England
Viking Penguin, a division of Penguin Books USA Inc.
375 Hudson Street, New York, New York 10014, USA
Penguin Books Australia Ltd, Ringwood, Victoria, Australia
Penguin Books Canada Ltd, 2801 John Street, Markham, Ontario, Canada L3R 1B4
Penguin Books (NZ) Ltd, 182–190 Wairau Road, Auckland 10, New Zealand

Penguin Books Ltd, Registered Offices: Harmondsworth, Middlesex, England

First published 1991
1 3 5 7 9 10 8 6 4 2

Text copyright © Kathryn Cave, 1991
Illustrations copyright © Stephen Player, 1991

Filmset in Linotron Palatino by Rowland Phototypesetting Ltd,
Bury St Edmunds, Suffolk

Printed in Great Britain by
Butler and Tanner Ltd, Frome, Somerset

A CIP catalogue record for this book is available from the British Library

ISBN 0–670–83487–4

Mary had a little lamb,
Its fleece was white as snow,
And everywhere that Mary went,
The lamb was sure to go.

One

The lamb trotted into William's life without warning one quiet Sunday. It wasn't his lamb, of course: it was Mary's. That's what happens, William thought, when you stuff a four-year-old with nursery rhymes. A grandmother should know better.

'Mary had a little lamb,' said the grandmother in question. She had one arm round Mary on the sofa. 'You didn't tell me that, Mary. Do you have a little lamb?'

Mary roared with laughter. William gritted his teeth.

'I'll ask William, shall I? William, does your sister really have a lamb hidden away somewhere?'

William turned a page without answering. He didn't want to be rude: the woman was his grandmother after all. On that very sofa she had once hugged him, and read him stories, and fed him fierce mints when his mother wasn't looking. That was a long time ago, when William was little. Before Mary.

William turned another page, expressionless.

'Do you have a little lamb, then, my darling?' More giggles from Mary. 'Where is it? Why don't you show it to me? Where does it live?'

Mary paused. If he hadn't known her, William might have said she was thinking. Then she pointed to the empty space at the end of the sofa. 'Over there, Grandma.'

'At the end of the sofa? Oh yes, I see it.'

There wasn't anything on the sofa. William could see it out of the corner of one eye and there was nothing there at all, not even a teddy bear. Only a big blue cushion.

'It looks to me as if it's asleep, Mary. Does it like to sleep there?'

'He always sleeps there.' Mary gave the blue cushion a pat that would have scared any animal out of its wits. A real lamb would have bitten her, William thought. A pity it wasn't a real one.

'Real lambs don't sleep on cushions,' said William to nobody in particular.

'He's not *on* the cushion,' said Mary. 'He's under it.'

'Anyone can see *that*,' said William's grandmother.

'They don't sleep under cushions either,' William observed without lifting his head.

'This lamb does,' said Mary. 'Anyway, he's not sleeping now. He's woken up.' She lifted the cushion and peered beneath it.

'What does it usually do when it wakes up?'

William winced. His grandmother had obviously made up her mind to be silly.

'He's a he, not an it,' Mary said. 'He has something to eat.'

'Grass, I expect,' said her grandmother.

'He eats mints, actually.'

'Mints? That's lucky.' William heard the click as his grandmother undid her handbag, then the rustle of paper.

'I'll give it to him.' Mary waved the mint over the space at the end of the sofa and then put it into her mouth.

'Lambs don't eat mints,' said William.

'Mine does. He's eaten it already. Now he wants another one.'

William's grandmother produced the roll of mints again. After Lamb had eaten two more, she offered the roll to William.

'No, thank you,' said William coldly. He rose, tucking the book under one arm. As he opened the door, Mary was announcing that Lamb wanted to play Snap.

'Snap?' William's grandmother didn't like card games, and she didn't like Snap more than anything William could think of. 'Wouldn't it rather play Snakes and Ladders?'

William lingered in the doorway.

'*He*,' said Mary, 'hates snakes. They give him bad dreams. So it'll have to be Snap, I'm afraid.'

'Oh well,' said his grandmother, putting a brave face on it. 'Better find the cards, then.'

William shut the door with grim satisfaction. His grandmother had been silly and she was going to pay for it. He went upstairs to read until tea-time.

When his mother called that tea was ready, William put aside his book and went swiftly downstairs. He knew that there were cup-cakes for tea and it was a simple matter to work out that if there were four people and eight cup-cakes, there would be two cup-cakes each. Maybe three for him, if Mary was only allowed one, and one was quite enough at her age.

But his father had come back from a trip to the garden centre, bringing William's grandfather with him. Six people: eight cup-cakes. William's hopes sank, but he helped himself and went over to the sofa.

'You can't sit there,' said Mary. 'That's Lamb's place.'

William put his plate on the arm of the sofa and sat down hard. The springs squeaked.

'You're sitting on Lamb!' Mary shrieked. 'You'll squash him!'

'William!' said his mother, his father and his grandmother in the same voice. His grandfather didn't join in because he had no idea what was going on. Anyway, he was taking a second cup-cake.

William got up and went to sit on the floor, as far away from everyone as possible. He ate quickly. There was still one cake left, and if he finished before his father, he would probably be allowed to take it.

'Lamb's hungry too.' The announcement came as William was chewing his last mouthful. 'Can he have the last cup-cake?'

'Are you sure he can manage it?' asked William's mother. 'All right then. You can feed it to him.'

Before William's eyes, Mary waved the cake over the blue cushion and then wolfed it down. It was gone, gone for ever.

William swallowed his mouthful. After it was gone, he cleaned the crumbs from his plate with a damp finger, doing his best not to see Mary putting on an act with the blue cushion: picking it up, stroking the air above it, making clucking noises.

'How's the football these days, William?' his grandfather asked. 'Still playing left –'

'Shush,' hissed Mary. 'Lamb's sleepy.'

'Yes, I'm still left wing,' said William loudly. 'SSSSSHHHH!'

William's grandmother laughed. 'They're a delight at that age, aren't they?' she murmured to William's mother. 'Such a shame they lose it as they get older.'

William got up. He knew when he was being insulted.

'Oh, William never had any imagination,' his mother said. 'Not even at her age. He was never a patch on Mary.'

'You'll have to take a leaf out of your sister's book, William,' said his grandfather in a heavy whisper. 'An invisible friend of your own, that's what you need. What sort will you have, eh? A lamb, like Mary's?'

William had no intention of replying. At that moment, anyway, he wasn't sure he could speak. Then his mother said 'William!' and he suddenly found that he could.

'No,' said William quietly from the doorway. 'I

won't have a lamb like Mary's. I'll have a wolf.'

Mary stopped stroking Lamb and looked up, faintly alarmed. Encouraged, William went on: 'Wolves, actually. Six of them. They'll be here first thing tomorrow.'

'Jolly good, William,' said his grandfather uneasily. 'Ha ha. Six wolves. Good joke.' Nobody else said anything.

'Goodbye Grandma and Grandpa,' William said when the silence had lasted long enough. 'Oh, and my wolves won't sleep on the sofa. They're timber wolves. They'll live in the garden shed. So you'd better move your bicycle, Mary, before they arrive.'

Smiling politely, William shut the door.

Two

William woke next morning pleased but puzzled. Something was going to happen, something he was looking forward to, but he couldn't think what. It wasn't his birthday or the first day of the holidays, or a Saturday. So why did he have the feeling that it was going to be a day to remember?

Next door his parents' bed creaked. William's father was getting up. Almost at once, Mary's feet pattered past William's door towards his parents' room. A small frown formed on William's face, and then vanished as he remembered what was going to make that Monday special: the wolves!

William threw back the quilt whistling.

'They're here,' he said at breakfast.

'What are?' asked his mother, yawning. 'Mary, Lamb *can't* have a chair all to himself, Daddy will need one. Lamb will have to sit on your lap instead.'

'But he keeps sliding off,' said Mary. 'And then he starts crying.'

'Put him on the sofa, then.' William's mother disappeared into the kitchen to make toast.

'But he's HUNGRY,' bellowed Mary. 'He hasn't had his cereal.'

'It's all right, Mary,' said William. 'Lamb can have my chair. I have to see to the wolves.'

'Wolves?' She sounded alarmed. A good beginning.

'In the shed. They'll be hungry too. And *they* don't eat cereal.'

14

Mary snatched Lamb off the chair and pressed him to her cardigan.

William rose, smiling pleasantly at his sister. 'Well, I'd better go and see what they're up to.'

At the door he stopped. 'Why don't you come too?' he asked. 'Bring Lamb if you want to.'

Mary shook her head and hugged Lamb tighter than ever.

'Watch through the window, then,' he said in a brotherly way. He left the room.

'Where are you off to?' asked William's mother.
'The shed.'

His mother said 'Oh' and went on scraping toast. Typical, thought William. Not a flicker of interest in

the wolves, not a glimmer – and yet she'd spend half the day chatting about Lamb to Mary. Still, it might be to his advantage in the long run.

Half-way down the back garden, William looked back at the house. Mary was kneeling on her chair, watching him through the window. He waved and went on to the shed. When he reached it, he opened the door and went swiftly in, shutting it fast behind him.

The shed was gloomy, its window overgrown with ivy. William sat on the table that ran along one side and looked around as he ate a mint he had found in his trouser pocket.

As a future home for six fully grown wolves, the shed was definitely on the small side. What with the bikes, the garden tools and the wheelbarrow, there was hardly space for one, let alone six. At a pinch, William supposed, four wolves could sleep on the table. The other two could curl up in the wheel-barrow. It was as well to get details like this worked out at the beginning.

There was a stack of flowerpots in the barrow. William moved them on to a shelf and put his father's gardening coat inside the barrow to pad the hard metal. He might not have imagination like Mary, but he knew how to make a wolf welcome.

Not one wolf, he reminded himself – six of them. Six wolves! And they'd said he had no imagination! He was only sorry he hadn't invented more: ten wolves, fifty, a hundred . . .

No, he could never have looked after so many. Six was a good number. Six wolves was plenty.

'William!' came a shout from outside. 'What are you doing? You'll be late for school.'

William jumped down from the table. On the way to the door he had an idea. Not a patch on Mary, eh? He'd show them. Watch this for pretending.

A minute later William opened the door a crack and squeezed out. His hair was tousled, his tie twisted under one ear. There was a streak of dirt on one cheek.

'Down!' he told the empty shed sternly. 'That's enough! I can't stay now. I'll be back this afternoon. Down, boys, *down*, I said.'

William banged the door and made something of a performance of pushing very hard to hold it shut while he put the latch down. He waved at Mary again and ran up the path to the house.

'For heaven's sake, William, go and wash your face. And hurry. We're late already.'

On his way to the bathroom, William stuck his head into the living-room. Mary was at the window, staring wide-eyed at the garden shed.

'They're all right,' William said. 'But they're very tired. They've come all the way from Siberia. Don't disturb them whatever happens. And keep Lamb out of the way: they've had quite enough to eat for one morning.'

'WILLIAM!'

'Have a nice day, Mary.' William ran.

Three

When he got home, Mary was in the kitchen, painting. The biscuit tin was on the table. William poured a drink and pushed back a chair.

'That's Lamb's place,' said Mary.

Not for long, William promised himself, not once the wolves got going. He opened the tin and took two chocolate biscuits. As he was about to close it, he thought again, and took four more.

'For the wolves,' he told Mary cheerfully. 'They'll be awake now. Of course, they'd prefer meat to biscuits. Fresh meat, tender meat, that's what wolves like. See you later, Mary. Oh, and look after Lamb, won't you?' William departed chuckling.

Really, he thought as he chewed biscuits in the musty darkness, it was almost too easy to fool someone like Mary, brought up on stupid fairy stories. She'd believe any old rubbish: talking wolves, wolves who dressed up as grandmothers. His wolves were going to be different. They'd be real animals: their fur ruffled by the wild north wind, their narrow eyes yellow and bright. Above all, they'd have no use for biscuits or cereal, having large business-like teeth. William's thoughts returned to Lamb. He shut his eyes and began to imagine Lamb's positively final appearance.

'William, where are you?'

At his mother's voice, William opened his eyes to find himself staring at the gardening coat in the wheelbarrow. It had toggles down the front instead of buttons – they didn't look as if they'd be comfortable to sleep on. Perhaps the wolves would bite them off? But then the coat would be ruined.

William frowned. There was more to this imagining business than he'd realized. He'd have to keep his wits about him. Could he cover the coat with the old rug from the spare room? Yes, that would work.

He had better fetch it right away, before he forgot.

'There you are,' William's mother said as he came through the kitchen door. 'No, don't disappear again. I've been looking for you for ages. Stay with Mary while I pop next door and borrow some milk from Mrs Evans, will you? We've run out.'

William pulled out the spare chair and sat down before Mary could say it was Lamb's place. To his disappointment, she didn't seem to care. He reminded her: 'Where's Lamb, then?'

'On the sofa. Watching television.'

Mary went on painting. William sneered. Television! You wouldn't catch his wolves wasting time on that. Oh, Lamb was doomed all right, no two ways about it.

As soon as his mother returned, William shot up to get the rug from the spare room.

'Where are you taking that, William?'

'The shed.'

'I suppose you're making a clubhouse or something.'

William said nothing. For one thing, there's no law against letting people suppose things, and for another, he was wondering where Mary had got to. Checking up on Lamb perhaps? But William was mistaken. Before he had reached the door to the garden, she was back in the kitchen, pale but determined, carrying the blue cushion.

'For the wolves,' she said, holding it out to William.

William was shocked, more than shocked: he was furious.

'Wolves don't sleep on cushions,' he said icily and slammed the door. He wouldn't put it past her to

follow him into the garden. Let her try, let her try, that's all, William told himself. Lambs weren't the only things a wolf could eat.

Seething, William strode down the path towards the shed. Only to stop dead after the first few yards.

He had shut the shed door behind him not half an hour ago, he was sure of it. But now the shed door was open.

Four

'For the last time, William,' said his mother, 'I did NOT open the shed door. And what does it matter if the door WAS open?'

'I'm doing something in the shed,' said William. 'It's private.'

'Then you'd better shut the door next time, hadn't you?'

'I DID shut it.'

'Don't shout, William.'

'How am I supposed to do anything when people keep poking around where they're not supposed to?'

'This is ridiculous, William. The door's shut now. It's not as if it makes any difference if it was open, does it?'

'You don't understand,' said William coldly, and stalked out of the kitchen.

Not make any difference, he thought bitterly, flinging himself on to the sofa. Of course it made a difference. If someone left the door open, what was to stop Mary looking in and seeing that there were no wolves there? Even if she didn't do that, how could he expect her to take the wolves seriously if no one else did? Why bother having wolves at all, William thought more bitterly still. They might as well be rabbits.

Mary came in. She put the cushion down and sat beside William. 'Where are the wolves?' she asked.

'How should I know?' William answered

savagely. 'The shed door was open. They could be anywhere.' Mary's eyes widened and her face became solemn. Slightly cheered, William turned up the menace: 'Anywhere!'

'In the garden?' Mary approached the patio window cautiously and peered at the back lawn. She *looked* as if she was still taking the wolves seriously all right.

William cheered up some more. 'They could be.'

Mary pressed her nose against the glass. 'In the bushes?'

'I expect so.'

'In the sand-pit?'

William hesitated. He didn't want Mary to think the wolves spent their time building sandcastles. 'I shouldn't worry about it,' he said, compromising.

Mary's forehead creased. It was her own sand-pit and she didn't let anyone use it, not even William – especially not William. And now, in her own sand-pit – wolves! Her lower lip quivered.

'Don't stand near the glass,' William said, to take her mind off. 'They don't have windows in Siberia. The wolves will think they can jump through and get you.'

'They won't be able to.'

'I don't *think* so,' said William generously.

Mary retreated behind the dining-room table. 'Wolves in the sand-pit,' she repeated, less sadly this time.

'Not necessarily,' said William quickly. It was definitely not up to Mary to decide where the wolves were. That was his department. 'They could be *anywhere*,' he reminded her. 'Among the rose-bushes. Behind the dustbins . . .'

'*In* the dustbins?'

'Yes – no. Maybe.' The interruption was not in William's script. 'No, not in the dustbins, there wouldn't be room for a wolf there. And it wouldn't like it. Not in the dustbins. Under the hedge . . .' William looked round the garden for ideas. 'On the . . . on the . . .'

'On the climbing-frame?'

'The climbing-frame? They're wolves, not chimpanzees!' William shouted.

'Are the chimpanzees on the climbing-frame, then?'

'There aren't any chimpanzees!'

'Why not?' asked Mary.

William took a deep breath. 'There are *no* chimpanzees,' he said, slowly and clearly. 'Not on the climbing-frame. Not anywhere else in the garden. There *are* wolves, and we don't know where they are. They could be anywhere!' He said this with all the menace he could manage.

Mary looked puzzled. 'The wolves are in the sand-pit,' she reminded him.

'No they're not!'

'Yes they are.'

'Whose wolves are they?' shouted William. 'Yours or mine?'

There was a pause.

'Your wolves, William,' said Mary softly.

'Go and see to Lamb,' said William in a furious voice. 'If the wolves find him, he's finished.'

'Yes, William.' But Mary was in no hurry. She lingered by the window, watching the sand-pit – or was it the climbing-frame? William hissed with exasperation.

'Well, go on. What are you waiting for?'

Mary gave one last look over her shoulder and moved slowly towards the sofa. It was victory of a sort, William supposed. He went off to the kitchen to get a drink.

Mary's voice floated after him. 'Don't worry about the wolves, Lamb,' she said, making a fuss of the blue cushion. 'Tomorrow you can play on the climbing-frame with the chimpanzees.'

William slammed the door.

Five

'There are wolves in the sand-pit,' Mary said at supper.

'There aren't,' said William grimly.

His father looked up, frowning. 'For heaven's sake, William. She's only pretending.'

'And chimpanzees on the climbing-frame.' Mary sent William a challenging glance.

Her mother gave an absent-minded smile. She hadn't been listening for the past five minutes. 'Really? Is that so?'

'No,' said William, louder. No one paid any attention.

'I'm going to let them share my celery. After Lamb's had some, of course.'

'Wolves don't eat celery!'

William's mother heard that all right. 'There's no need to shout, William.'

'They can eat celery if they want to,' said Mary. 'And chimpanzees love it.' She pushed the celery to the side of her plate. 'Can I get down now?'

'No,' said her mother. 'That celery is for you, not

Lamb or anyone else. No pudding until it's finished.'

Mary sulked for the rest of the meal. So did William. But by the time he'd had pudding, he could see what had to be done.

First, get rid of the chimpanzees, who had no business on the climbing-frame or anywhere else, and were being a thorough nuisance.

Second, get the wolves back in the shed, and put a stop to all argument over where they were and what they were up to.

Third, make it clear once and for all that wolves are not keen on vegetables. William was looking forward to this bit. He had Lamb in mind for a brief but interesting role.

'I'm going to call the wolves in for the night,' William said to Mary when his parents went to clear up the kitchen. 'Watch through the window if you like. Don't make a noise, though. Wolves are funny about noises. They're funny about chimpanzees too. It's a good thing there aren't any about or things could get *very* nasty.' He gave Mary a hard look.

'The chimpanzees have gone,' said Mary. 'They went when they couldn't have my celery. Can I see the wolves now?'

'You can look, but they're very hard to see at this time of night. That's why they're such good hunters. Make sure Lamb doesn't follow me into the garden.'

Mary nodded, eyes like saucers. William slipped out through the patio window.

'Ssshhh!' he mimed from the terrace. Mary nodded again. William smiled and set off through the twilight. Down by the shed, he opened the door and gave a soft whistle. 'Here, wolf,' he called into the shadows. Mary probably couldn't hear, but she might see his lips move. 'Come here, boy.'

A shape loomed up suddenly on the other side of the hedge, giving William a nasty turn.

'Have you lost something, William?'

Mrs Evans from next door. William grunted and went on poking the hedge. He could hardly find six

wolves with her watching. He only hoped she'd go in before Mary saw her.

'A pussy cat, is it, William?' Mrs Evans asked, sticking her head over the hedge.

William crouched lower and pretended to peer down the gap between the hedge and the shed. A pussy cat! What did she think he was? But Mrs Evans was slow to take the hint. She leaned right over the hedge to peer into the garden.

'Come kitty, kitty, kitty!' she called. 'Puss-wuss-wuss!'

That settled it as far as William was concerned. No self-respecting wolf was going to go tamely back into the shed while Mrs Evans was there, absolutely crying out to be eaten. The pity was, William could see no way to arrange it. Imagination can take you just so far and no further. On the other hand, maybe it could do the trick after all . . .

'It's not a cat, Mrs Evans. It's my grass snakes. I let them out for a run, you see, and they came this way. They must have slithered through the hedge. Can you see if – ?'

There was a shriek and Mrs Evans was gone. William lost no time in hauling the first wolf out of the privet.

'Bad wolf,' he said indulgently. 'You can't eat Mrs Evans. Not yet. Into the shed with you – and you too, both of you.'

So – three wolves rounded up already, and three to go. Plus the grass snakes. It wouldn't do to forget them. Mrs Evans was probably following his every move from her upstairs back-window.

William fetched a large flowerpot from the shed and groped around in the shadow beneath the

30

hedge. One snake. Two snakes. Three snakes, nice and wriggly. He thought of pretending to find a fourth, but time was short and he had a lot to see to. He wiped his fingers on his trousers and carried the pot back to the shed. He put it on a high shelf, out of the reach of wolves.

Now, on with the wolf-catching. The compost heap was next on his list of places wolves might be lurking – two wolves, he rather thought. He waved at Mary and strolled across the garden, clicking his fingers. 'Come out, wolves, wherever you are. Ah!'

There was a pile of grass clippings at the back of the heap. William crouched down beside it and scratched the air at what he thought would be wolf-head height. 'Good wolf, beautiful wolf. Home to the shed, both of you. It won't be for long, I promise.'

William strode back across the garden, feeling every inch the master of a pack of wolves.

Now there was only one wolf left. While William was making up his mind where to find it, a sharp noise made him turn towards the house: Mary rapping on the window.

He waved impatiently – 'SSSHHH!' – but the rapping grew louder. Mary was looking alarmed, pointing at the sand-pit.

'WHAT DO YOU WANT?' mouthed William, exasperated. It takes a lot out of you, catching invisible wolves. There's nothing worse than constant interruptions.

'IT'S IN THE SAND-PIT,' Mary mouthed back through the glass.

The cheek of it took William's breath away.

'IT IS NOT!' Scowling, William stalked over to the sand-pit. 'LOOK!' He levered up one side of the lid and peered in. It was too dark to see inside, but that didn't matter. He let the lid fall and stood up again. 'THERE'S NOTHING THERE.'

Three faces stared back at him through the window, wearing expressions of amazement and disbelief.

'William!' His father opened the window. 'Have you gone mad? It's far too late to play in the sand-pit! Come in this minute.'

'Look at your feet!' said his mother. 'Those socks were only on this morning. Go and put them in the washing-basket at once.'

'Can't I just–'

'NO!' said his parents together.

That was that. The last wolf would have to wait. He couldn't leave the shed door, though. Five wolves was better than none.

'Just a minute.' William raced down the path to the shed before anyone could say no. 'Be good, wolves,' he told the darkness. 'I'll be back tomorrow, I promise.' He wasn't sure what to say to the grass snakes. Sleep tight? Sweet dreams? What would a grass snake dream *of*?

'William!'

'Coming.' When he tried to shut the shed door, it was stiff. He had to put his shoulder to it, and even then it closed reluctantly, with a noise like an animal whining. William clicked the latch down, disconcerted.

'Hurry UP!' his father called again.

William ran.

An hour later, he lay in his dark room, eyes open. A wind had sprung up outside. Trees creaked, leaves rustled, and somewhere close at hand a door was banging. A door?

Throwing back the quilt, William knelt up and pulled aside one curtain. The lid of the sand-pit had blown off and was half-way down the garden. The

33

shed door was swinging in the moonlight.

They were out again!

William's heart sank as he thought of all the rounding-up to be done next morning. Unless he could wake early and shut the shed door before anyone found out it had been open . . .?

Yes, that was the way to get things under control. It was vital to wake early.

But as he fell asleep he heard the wind howling, and he dreamed that the wolves ran free.

Six

A few breaths later, William woke to Mary's voice in his left ear.

'The wolves are out again!'

'Uh?' William hoped he was dreaming.

'The shed's open!'

'Uhhummf?' Not a dream, a nightmare.

'And the lid's blown off the sand-pit, so they're not in there.'

'Arharmawhumf?' This was the closest William could get to 'Is it morning?'

'That's just what I said,' Mary said triumphantly. 'They could be *anywhere*! I'd better go and see Lamb's all right.'

'Fliffle Lah,' said William from the bottom of his heart.

'I *know*,' said Mary from the doorway. '*And* the chimpanzees are back. They're on the climbing-frame. I've seen them!'

'What!?' cried William, waking up suddenly. 'WHAT??'

The day had begun.

By the time William had pulled on his clothes, stuffed his feet into shoes and reeled downstairs, Mary was at the table having breakfast. The blue cushion was on the chair beside her – William's chair. It was where he always sat.

William looked at the blue cushion. Then he stalked to the patio window. 'Poor chimpanzees,' he said. 'I suppose the wolves got them?'

'What do you mean?' Mary had been tearing the crusts off her toast to give to Lamb. Now she looked up. 'The wolves didn't get them.'

'Where have they gone, then?' William sounded surprised. 'I mean, they're not here now.' He waved a hand at the garden. It was empty – anyone could see that.

'They might be hiding.' Mary tumbled off her chair and raced to the window. 'Look over –'

'They've gone,' said William very firmly. 'They saw the wolves and they left. A good thing too: the wolves will be starving and there's nothing they like better than chimpanzee for breakfast.' He didn't like saying the last bit – he knew wolves didn't eat breakfast – but he had to get the point across some-how.

Cornered, Mary became defiant. 'How do *you* know?'

'They're my wolves,' said William distantly. 'I know that sort of thing. You wouldn't understand.'

'I would!'

'Then you'll understand that the chimpanzees won't be coming back, won't you?' said William with what he thought was fiendish cunning.

He hadn't allowed for Mary's stubbornness: 'They *will* come back. We're going to have a tea-party.'

'If they come back, the wolves will eat them,' William snapped.

Mary's face fell. She wasn't ready to give up, though. 'They mightn't eat all of them,' she said.

'Yes, all of them. Every single one. *And* the tea-set too.' William thought the tea-set would do the trick, if nothing else did. Mary was horribly fond of tea-parties.

'I don't care if they do,' said Mary. 'I'm going to use the set I don't like.' She pointed to a stack of yellow plastic cups at the end of the table.

William was speechless. Then: 'I gave you those!' he shouted. (This wasn't strictly true: his mother had bought the tea-set the day before Mary's last birthday, which he had forgotten, as usual. William hadn't actually chosen it, or wrapped it, or paid for it, but for all Mary knew, he might have.) He was cut to the quick.

'They're my second-best ones,' said Mary comfortingly. 'I *almost* like them.' She sat down again and started tearing up paper handkerchiefs to use as food at the party.

William took his father's chair and fumed in

silence through two slices of toast. As he reached for
the third, his eye lighted on a small round object at
the edge of the lawn. A flowerpot? It must have
blown out of the shed in the night. Why did it look
so familiar? Ha! With a rush, William remembered
the grass snakes.

'Be careful, won't you?' he said in a casual tone,
reaching for the butter. 'I mean, it isn't just
the wolves, you know.' He buttered the toast,
whistling.

'What isn't just the wolves?' asked Mary, inter-
ested. 'You mean the chimpanzees aren't?'

William counted to ten. He must not allow himself to be sidetracked. 'There are the snakes as well.
Don't forget them, will you?'

'What snakes?'

'My snakes, of course. I was telling Mrs Evans
about them last night. You saw us talking, didn't
you? That proves it. The snakes were in a flowerpot
in the shed, and when the door blew open, they

escaped. They're on the lawn somewhere, I expect.'

'Go and catch them at *once*,' said Mary.

'I don't have time.' William rose from the table. 'But don't worry. I *think* they're grass snakes. I'll look them up in the library to make sure. Let me know if they bite you, won't you? Because if they do, then they aren't – grass snakes, that is.'

The next time William passed the door, Mary was waiting. 'What happens if a snake that isn't a grass snake bites you?'

'I don't know, Mary.' William smiled tenderly. 'You tell me. You're the one who's going to play in the garden with them.' He went to pack his bag.

'Do wolves eat snakes?' Mary asked when he passed through to pick up his lunch-box.

'Only when they've eaten everything else – chimpanzees, Lambs and so forth,' said William airily. 'Well, I must be off. All the best to Lamb and the chimpanzees, in case something happens to them while I'm gone. And don't forget: I need to know exactly what the snakes do, who they bite, where, and how often. Enjoy the tea-party, Mary. See you after school.'

But his feeling of triumph had faded by the time he reached the bus-stop. After school there would be wolves to round up, snakes to collect, chimpanzees to keep out of the garden. It was a full-time job, all this pretending.

But it would be worth it, William thought as he climbed on to the bus. When Lamb got what was coming to him, it would be worth every minute.

Seven

The next few days passed in a blur for William – days filled with planning, evenings with hard work. He had so much to get done: wolves to feed, snakes to water, chimpanzees to hold at bay, Mary to terrify. He was succeeding, he thought. Definitely succeeding.

'Look what one of the wolves did when I put it back in the shed just now,' William said on Tuesday evening. He gave a theatrical wince as he pulled up his left trouser-leg. His shin, never a pretty sight, was looking worse than usual because he had been pushed over at school by a huge fourth-year called Brewster. Mary didn't know about that, though.

'Look at those claw marks! See those holes where it used its teeth?' William went on with relish. 'It was only playing, of course. It didn't mean to hurt me.'

Mary turned pale. 'It was only playing,' she repeated fervently. 'It's a *nice* wolf.'

'A *very* nice wolf. They all are.' William let the trouser-leg down and went up to his room satisfied.

Next day, though, something peculiar happened. 'Bad Lamb,' said Mary in the middle of breakfast. '*Don't* bite Teddy. Whatever has got into you today?'

It wasn't worrying, exactly. William definitely wasn't worried. He spent the whole bus ride to school not worrying about it in the slightest.

'Look!' said Mary, thrusting her arm under

William's nose as soon as he got home that after-noon.

The arm looked all right to William. He said so, and added a few words on having enough to do as it was without people waving arms in his face the moment he came home from school and if she wouldn't mind moving he'd like a biscuit.

'Lamb bit me. *Me!*' said Mary tragically.

William shut his eyes. He tried to shut his ears too, but that was harder.

'And then he *ate* Sylvia.' That was Mary's smallest teddy bear. 'And when I told him to say sorry, he said fliffle Sylvia, he was hungry!'

'Fliffle?' asked William. He couldn't help it.

'He said it, not me,' said Mary with disapproval.

At that moment, William was particularly glad that he knew he was succeeding. The alternative didn't bear thinking about.

The pretending was such a performance, too. The imaginary plates of raw meat the wolves ate . . . the buckets of water. The mess they made of the flowerbeds, or the mess William made for them. He didn't like doing it, he had nothing against daffodils, but wolves will be wolves. They don't have flowerbeds in Siberia.

'If I catch you trampling my flowers once more, there'll be trouble,' shouted William's father on Wednesday evening. 'I spent over ten pounds on those bulbs. Now look at them!'

'It was the wolves,' said William.

'Don't give me that,' said his father. Not a word about William being so imaginative and such a delight to his parents. Just 'Keep off my plants or you'll lose a month's pocket money, and that's only

the beginning.' As if you could keep six wolves in a small garden without some drop in standards . . . Now William had to make sure the wolves watched where they were treading as well as all his other labours.

Thank heavens for snakes, William thought. Snakes were easy. They kept the garden free of chimpanzees (and Mrs Evans) and at night they slept in the sand-pit. Mary didn't seem to mind – she even left the sand-pit lid off so the snakes could get in and out on their own via a small ramp William had built up to the terrace.

On Friday morning she saw the snakes using it.

William had to say he saw them too, right in the middle of breakfast. He would have lost face if he hadn't.

'Purple snakes!' said Mary, delighted.

'Brown ones,' said William drenchingly.

'I meant brown. Look at them, all lovely and wriggly!'

William would have liked to say they weren't wriggly either, but snakes were, so he couldn't. It put him right off his cornflakes.

His mother buttonholed him as he was leaving the house. 'I want a word with you, William.' More trouble.

'I don't want any more of this S-N-A-K-E nonsense,' she whispered fiercely. 'You'll give her bad dreams.'

'Me? That's a laugh.' William laughed hollowly.

'It's no laughing matter. If you had a scrap of imagination, you'd see that. Going on about wolves. Pretending to see snakes. The past few days I don't know what's got into you.'

'She's the only one who's allowed to see things, is she?' William shouted. 'I'm not, is that it?'

'It's different for her. She gets carried away. She believes the stories she makes up. You can't tell me you do, William. Well?' William glared at his mother. 'Are you going to tell me you believe the ridiculous stories you've been filling her head with?'

William couldn't believe his ears. Ridiculous? He was too flabbergasted to speak.

'It's got to stop,' his mother finished, more calmly. 'Now get a move on or you'll miss the bus.'

William reeled down the path. Stop seeing his beautiful wolves – never!

Hang on, a voice said somewhere inside him. You never have actually seen them, have you? Or the snakes either, come to that. Mary had seen them. If he didn't get a move on, she'd beat him to it and see the wolves first too.

It mustn't happen, William was absolutely determined. He would see the wolves at the first opportunity. Right away. That very morning.

'And then I'll see the snakes too. I'll show them who's best at imagining,' said William grimly. 'I'll show them all.'

Eight

On the bus, William took a window seat on the top deck to make wolf-spotting easier. Not that it ought to be difficult, as far as he could see. All it took was imagination, and he had just as much of that as Mary. More, probably. This was the time to prove it.

William leant forward and narrowed his eyes. Where would a timber wolf most like to be on a brisk May morning? Not down there in the swimming-pool, that looked far too cold. What about the springboard, though? It was a perfect spot for sun-bathing. William narrowed his eyes further and squinted hopefully at the board. He could almost see a wolf sprawling across it, legs dangling, eyes half-closed . . .

Almost. The bus creaked into first gear. It was no good fooling himself. The pool was deserted.

So was the supermarket car-park. William looked so hard for wolves under an enormous delivery van that his eyes crossed and the woman sitting next to him moved to another seat. Nothing. Well, super-markets were boring. He wasn't surprised wolves avoided them. But would the other places on his bus route be any better?

Feeling slightly desperate, William willed the wolves to appear immediately on the steps outside the Civic Centre. OK, it wasn't very exciting but they were his wolves and they owed him some-thing.

'Just for a minute,' he begged them silently,

'that's all. A quick prowl across the steps. You're mine, aren't you? So let me see you. Is that too much to ask?'

It was. He stared till his head ached and his eyes watered. Nothing. Not a sausage.

Thanks a lot, William thought bitterly as the bus bumped off down the High Street. I'll do the same for you one day.

He shut his smarting eyes – not giving up, not by any means. He wasn't finished yet. He was going to see those wolves if it killed him, if it –

Suddenly William stiffened. With no warning at all, there they were! Not just six wolves either – twenty of them, fifty, more like a hundred . . . And

who was that there with them? William screwed his eyes shut more tightly. Was it, could it be . . .?

Yes! The person with the wolves was he himself. It was William!

He saw himself in a sledge, urging his horses across a frozen waste while the wolves streamed out behind him like an army, wild and free. Flick – one touch on a switch William didn't even know he had – and all at once he was looking down from a balcony in a castle, while his army in the courtyard lifted their muzzles to the moon and howled. Flick. There was a banquet spread before him in a great hall where the firelight sent wolf shadows leaping across the walls.

'Wake up, lad. Let's see your ticket. I haven't got all day.'

William kept his eyes shut as he fumbled in his pocket. Far away a wolf growled menacingly. Little did the inspector know, William thought, with whom he was dealing. He had to open one eye though, to check he had the right ticket.

'About time.' The inspector sniffed ferociously and passed on. 'Tickets, please.'

Alone again – as much as you can be on a bus in the rush hour – William shut his eyes and reached for the secret switch. Flick. But instead of the castle, all it produced was a building that reminded William of the Civic Centre. The balcony looked out

over the High Street. There wasn't a wolf to be seen.

William opened his eyes again, puzzled. Perhaps people with imagination have to expect setbacks now and then. Perhaps even Mary couldn't see what she wanted to every time. It was annoying, though, when things had been going so brilliantly.

The bus was picking up speed as it left the town centre. Shops and houses slipped by without William noticing, until he found himself looking at a park with well-cut lawns, tidy trees, an empty playground. A council worker with a rake was the only person in sight. A couple of Alsatians were sniffing round the slide.

Then – and this happened so quickly that William wasn't sure he had truly seen it – as the bus drew level with them, the dogs lifted their heads and looked at William with yellow eyes. Dogs? He blinked, and as if at a signal, they turned and loped across the grass towards the man with the rake.

Already the bus was leaving the playground behind. William twisted in his seat to see the animals covering the ground with deadly speed. The man could see them coming. He dropped his rake. He was climbing a tree. The bus swept round a corner. They were gone.

'Who are you staring at?' said a girl in the seat behind, a fourth-former. 'Do you mind!'

William turned back, thoughts racing. Had it happened? Had he really seen them at last? He was almost sure of it. Almost? He *was* sure. He and nobody else had actually *seen* the wolves.

Two of them, anyway. William felt it would be better to see them all. It would wrap things up, somehow. He must keep looking.

And when the bus stopped at the next set of traffic-lights, there they were – down a side-street, investigating a milk-float.

How easily they dodged the bottles that the milk-man flung at them, how beautifully they leapt and twisted, pausing every now and then to drink from the gutter. Their tails were waving. They were enjoying themselves. William was less sure about the milkman. He was down to his last crate of bottles and the wolves were getting closer. Closer . . . The lights changed.

At the school stop, William followed the crowd down the stairs and jumped off. Half-way to the junior-school entrance, an interesting thought struck him. He looked over his shoulder.

There was a wolf at the railings. Two wolves . . . three. While William hesitated, the rest slunk up, speckled with milk and panting. The last wolf was dragging a milkman's satchel. When it saw William, it dropped the bag and jumped up against the railings, whining.

William knew what it wanted. 'Oh, all right, then,' he said. 'But I don't want any trouble. Understand?'

The school-bell rang. William held the door open for the wolves and went inside.

Nine

It's trickier than you'd think, managing an imaginary wolf pack – trickier than William expected, anyway. He could see the wolves. Other people couldn't. It sounded straightforward enough.

The first inkling William had of problems came when he bumped into Brewster, huge and horrible, in the corridor outside class. William did what anyone would have: there's no point having wolves if you don't use them.

'OK,' whispered William. '*Get* him!'

Off went the wolves like thunderbolts. Off went the imaginary Brewster, shrieking, swearing, wailing.

It was a wonderful chase – up stairs, along corridors, the full length of the library. One wolf managed a passing bite at Mrs Rattigan, terror of the middle school – William cheered. Then on they swept, scattering teachers like leaves in autumn. Almost too soon they had Brewster cornered in the science block, on top of a display-case of prehistoric Bunsen burners. Crash! the case collapsed. Brewster cowered amid the splinters as his pursuers closed in, panting –

'Watch who you're pushing, Johnson.'

William blinked in surprise. The real Brewster, knuckles bulging, was flourishing a huge fist. 'Or you'll find out what it's like to be pushed –' He gave a demonstration. William staggered. '*Hard* –'

'Ow!' Where were the wolves now he needed

them? Far away, ripping their imaginary victim limb from limb. While the real Brewster got into his stride.

'And then let's see how you like it.'

Thud thud THUD. William hit a wall, a classroom door, a floor – all real ones. And it wasn't the wolves who saved him: it was Mr Turner, his form teacher. Not that it felt like being saved. Even in a good mood Mr Turner didn't so much speak as bellow. And he was never in a good mood first thing.

'What do you think you are DOING, boy? Is this a gymnasium? Is it a circus? Is it a MUSIC hall?

Have you gone raving MAD? Why don't you answer me, boy? What's the matter with you?'

'Winded,' William gasped faintly.

'Winded, SIR,' roared Mr Turner.

The classroom windows rattled. Two floors away the headmaster jumped like a startled deer, spilling his cup of herbal tea. In the far-off science block, the wolves flattened their ears and scattered. William had no time to see where they went. Mr Turner was off again.

'And WHY are you winded? I'll tell you why. You are winded because you, like all the other children in this class, are desperately unfit. When I was your age, I ran five miles every morning before breakfast. I could do fifty press-ups. Can you do fifty press-ups? Go on, try, boy. Over on your front, hands beneath your shoulders. Right! Now straighten your arms. We'll see how fit you are.'

With a superhuman effort, William straightened his arms. The floor fell away beneath him. Desperately unfit, eh? He'd show them. But the second time he tried it, he found himself eyeball to eyeball with a wolf. It wagged its tail and dropped something on the floor in front of him – a piece of material badly chewed and mangled, stained with blood. The sleeve of a blazer? Brewster's blazer! With awful suddenness, the floor rose up and struck William painfully on the nose.

'Call that a press-up?' scoffed Mr Turner. 'You've got no muscles, none of you. No wonder we didn't win a netball match all winter.'

'I'm dot od the detball teeb, sir.' William's nose was hurting. He couldn't see the wolf. Where had it gone to?

'I'm not surprised. You wouldn't make the tiddly-winks team, the state you're in. Well, don't just lie on the floor snuffling, what's-your-name. Go and sit down. You're late.'

William slunk to his seat, seriously rattled. Things were not going as he'd expected. Wolves there one minute, gone the next. Not coming when he called them, then coming when he didn't. It was enough to fluster anyone. He needed a breathing space to collect his thoughts.

Concentrating hard, William shut his eyes and tried to picture the wolves having a quiet rest where no one would disturb them, like behind the games shed or in the reference section of the library. If he could just park them there, so to speak, until break, he'd have time to work out what was going on. William screwed his eyes shut more tightly.

'Wake UP in the back row there. Yes YOU, boy.'

William opened his eyes. Mr Turner was glaring at him. A wolf was glaring at Mr Turner.

'Well, boy?'

The wolf growled deep in its throat and advanced stiff-legged towards Mr Turner's ankle. It was too much. William folded up in his seat and tried to disappear.

'What is the MATTER with you, boy? Have you got chestnut blight? Is your tie caught in your TROUSERS?'

Breaking into a light sweat, William uncurled a trifle.

'LOOK at me when I am speaking to you, boy! What have you to say for yourself? Nothing? Then pay attention in future. I'm watching you.'

Mr Turner watched William. William watched the wolf. The wolf chewed what was left of Brewster's blazer. Of the three of them, the wolf seemed happiest. Its tail swept to and fro across the floor, raising a puff of dust with each stroke. Sweep puff. Sweep puff. They ought to sweep the floor more often, William thought. But at least the wolf was settling down. Maybe that was what it needed – what all of them needed. A little peace, a little understanding . . .

His dream was rudely interrupted by the bell.

'ASSEMBLY,' cried Mr Turner in a voice of doom.

The wolf's tail froze.

'Line up behind me at the door in absolute SILENCE! You too, William, IF you would be so good.'

Mr Turner set off towards the door. The third step he took landed heavily on the wolf's tail. A yelp, a snarl, a flurry of feet, and it was gone like a rocket. There was nothing William could do to stop it.

'ARE you coming to assembly this morning, William? Then HURRY UP! Thank you. Right, if everyone is ready at LAST, off we GO!'

There was no alternative. With the deepest misgivings, William went.

Ten

William found it difficult to remember the rest of that Friday properly. He never forgot it either, though, however hard he tried. Some things you never do forget.

The wolves in assembly, for instance – chewing Mr Turner's shoelaces . . . ambushing late arrivals in the senior cloakroom . . . sneaking along the curtain at the back of the platform while the Head made announcements . . . There was the howling that broke out when Miss Simms started to play 'All Things Bright and Beautiful', the menacing advance upon the piano . . . his own fatal moment of panic. There was the interview with the Head afterwards . . . the questions that had no answers.

'What has poor Miss Simms ever done to you, William? What has she done to anyone, come to that? She may not be the world's best pianist, but she was doing her best. Jumping up like that! Shouting "Go home" only inches from her left ear in the middle of verse three! She has gone home, William, and I for one cannot blame her. What on earth possessed you to behave in such an inconsiderate fashion? Sorry? I should hope you are, William. I should hope you are.'

The Head went on like this for ages and William missed morning break. He missed break at lunchtime too, but that wasn't because of the Head.

'I have had more than enough from you today, William,' said Mr Turner. 'Was that your idea of being funny? What WAS it then?'

William said nothing. It seemed the best policy in the circumstances.

'Right, let's take it slowly.' When Mr Turner spoke as quietly as this it was a bad sign. 'It was the middle of the fifth period. Long division. Everything normal – even you, if I remember correctly. The sun was shining, the birds were singing, and the only thing to complain about was that the classroom was perhaps a little stuffy. Are you with me, William?'

William nodded. No problems so far.

'Good. Now, because it was a little stuffy, I decided to open a window. I went over to the window by my desk and opened it wide. I leant out to take a breath of air. And that's where you came in, William, wasn't it?'

William nodded again, less happily. There was no getting away from it. It was.

'For some reason best known to yourself, you chose that moment to shout at the top of your voice "Watch out!" Now, why did you do that, William?'

For a split second William pondered whether or not to tell the truth: there was this wolf sneaking up behind you, sir, and I was worried what might happen . . . No, it was out of the question.

'I only meant be careful, sir.'

'I WAS being careful, William. Until you shouted, I was as careful as could be. Only WHEN you shouted, I straightened up and hit my head on the window-frame. And before I spend my lunch-hour in hospital getting the cut stitched, I would like to know WHAT ON EARTH YOU WERE THINKING OF??? Have you ANYTHING to

say for yourself?'

At that moment William hadn't.

But later on, when he was writing 'I must think
before I speak' fifty times during lunch-break, he felt
like saying, well, but what about the wolf? It wasn't
much fun for it either. Getting trodden on all over
again. It was still limping. William could see it at that

moment, under Mr Turner's desk, licking its paw and growling. You couldn't say it looked a happy wolf.

By the end of the afternoon, no one was looking happy, least of all William.

Usually he enjoyed football. He was good at it. Not that afternoon, though.

'Play!' shouted Mr Potter, blowing his whistle.

It wasn't play the wolves had in mind by the look of it. William was rooted to the spot. Even so, he couldn't help admiring the way they sneaked up on Mr Potter while he was coaching the reserve goal-keeper: what efficiency, what brilliant teamwork. Aha! Mr Potter had seen them too! Too late!

The ring of wolves closed in, tighter, tighter . . . With a heroic effort, Mr Potter leapt for the crossbar. Yes! He was up there. He was safe.

Balked of their first victim, the wolves turned towards the group of boys huddled in terror at the far end of the pitch. Who could save them now? William.

Quelling all panic by his mere presence, William ordered everyone to remove shin-guards and form a circle facing outwards. Using the shin-guards to hold the wolves at bay, the players edged their way towards the cloakroom. Only a few yards more, only a few inches –

'WILLIAM!'

'Yes, Mr Potter?' said William absently.

'That's the third pass you've missed. What is the matter with you?'

The real Mr Potter was glaring. The real football players were not gazing at William with admiration. The real William was not a hero.

When the game finished, he wasn't on the football team either.

'It's all your fault,' William told the wolves as he made his way back to the cloakroom, thoroughly fed up. 'Get lost!'

They blinked their yellow eyes and slunk furtively into school at his heels.

'What am I to say to you, William?' asked the Head half an hour later. 'What am I to say?'

William was past caring.

'That business with Miss Simms this morning. The accident to Mr Turner. And now this.'

At least he didn't know about the football game.

'It was quite deliberate too, in my opinion.' Mrs Rattigan glared at William from beside the Head. 'He deliberately swerved into my path and made me spill my cup of coffee all over myself.'

'Well, William?'

'I didn't mean to.'

'He had absolutely no reason to jump over to my side of the corridor. There was nothing in his way. Nobody was coming from the other direction.'

William looked up, and then down again at the carpet. There was no point trying to explain about the wolf. It had bounded out so suddenly from the staffroom, dragging Mr Potter by the ankle. Of course William had swerved towards Mrs Rattigan. Anyone would have. It's not the sort of thing you expect at 3.15 on a Friday. But who was going to believe him? Not Mrs Rattigan, and not the Head.

'I am disappointed in you, William. Very disappointed. You seemed such a sensible boy up to now, so level-headed. Are you having problems here? At home, maybe?'

William thought of mentioning Lamb. No, it was too complicated. The Head would never understand.

'No, sir.'

'Then let's have no more of this nonsense, William. Apologize to Mrs Rattigan and go home. And do better in future. Do you understand me?'

'Yes, sir.'

William kicked a stone moodily across the play-ground. He'd missed break. He'd missed his lunch. He'd missed his bus. He'd lost his place on the football team. The day had been one long disaster. Do better in future? The tricky thing would be to do worse.

The stone hit the gate and skidded towards the bus-stop. William's eyes followed it, brooding. As he saw it, people talked a lot of rubbish about imagination. It was ridiculously overrated. He was in a position to say, once and for all, that what imagination caused was trouble. At the first oppor-tunity he was going to abandon it for ever.

Not yet, however. First, there was a little matter of unfinished business: the beginning of the whole disaster, the cause of it all . . .

'Lamb!' muttered William. The time for the final reckoning had come.

The bus swept up. Deep in thought, William picked his way through the tired wolves and climbed on board.

Eleven

William's plans for the rest of the afternoon were simple. A rest. A light snack. A little scene-setting for Mary's benefit. Then – goodbye Lamb for ever. William smiled as he headed for the sofa.

Mary let out a shriek. 'Don't sit there!'

William's smile froze. 'Lamb's place, is it?' he snarled wearily. No doubt about it: the sooner the wolves got going the better. The world without Lamb would be a cleaner, happier place.

'No, it's not Lamb. The snakes are under the cushion. Not that one, the red one. *Don't* look. They're sleeping.'

A world without snakes too, William decided, collapsing on to a chair. But that could wait. Lamb came first. He would have to begin by establishing the whereabouts of the blue cushion. Carefully casual, William put the question to Mary.

'Lamb? Oh, he's outside,' said Mary.

'*Outside???*' William couldn't believe his ears. The carelessness of it, the sheer stupidity!

'Playing in the shed.'

'But what about the wolves?' William shouted. 'Go and get him, you stupid girl.'

'I can't,' said Mary, perking up tremendously. 'I'm frightened. I think the wolves are coming.'

'They're not!'

'They are, they are!' Mary wrung her hands – rather well for someone with so little practice.

'They'll eat Lamb for tea, every bit of him. Even his hoofs.'

'No they won't!' William was sure about that. He had not gone through so much only to see Lamb perish accidentally, for heaven's sake. Where would the satisfaction be in that? 'Wolves don't have tea.' But Mary wasn't listening.

'Oh, all right,' said William, exasperated. 'I'll get him for you. Just this once, mind you. The wolves won't hurt me.'

All the same, it felt peculiar, and not entirely pleasant, entering the gloom of the shed. The cushion was on the floor under the wheelbarrow. When he picked it up, William had the impression something growled at him. He made a hasty exit.

The door wouldn't shut properly again. As he fumbled with the latch, something stirred in the bushes close by. Probably a cat, William thought. A big cat. More like a dog, really, or even a . . . William gave up on the door and scuttled back to the house.

He gave the cushion back to Mary, along with a lecture on looking after Lamb better in future. 'You can't expect other people to run round rescuing him,' he finished severely. 'He's your responsibility.'

'Yes, William.'

William evicted the red cushion from the sofa and lay down. His plans for Lamb needed a few finishing touches. Mary would be on her guard now, so it would be harder to lure her away from Lamb long enough to let the wolves do their stuff, but William didn't mind this. It gave him more scope for cunning. Mary was no match for him there. William's eyes closed.

The sound that woke him was a familiar one, but at first William didn't recognize it. A heavy swishing noise – something sliding? He sat up.

Mary was standing by the patio window. Ah, that was what the noise was. She must have opened the window while he was asleep, gone outside, and come back in again. Why, William wondered. He yawned and strolled across to the window.

'Seen any wolves?' he asked.

'Not yet.' Mary went on looking at the garden.

'They're there,' said William smugly. Who was the one with imagination now, eh? 'Can't you see that one sticking its head through the shed door? Or that one on the compost heap? Surely you can see the one by the rose-bush?'

'Which rose-bush?'

'At the end. Look where I'm pointing. The one by the daffodils, right beside the –' William broke off in horror.

'By Lamb, you mean?' asked Mary. 'By the blue cushion?'

'How did he get out again?' William shouted. 'Can't you look after him for five minutes?'

'He must have run out.'

'Run out!' William fumbled with the catch of the windows. There was no time to lose. Any minute the wolf would see Lamb and wreck William's dreams of revenge for ever. 'It's the last time I do this for you, understand? He's your Lamb, not mine. Next time you jolly well save him yourself.'

'Yes, William.'

William slid the window shut and set off down the garden seething. Some people didn't deserve to have animals. Look at the way Mary treated Lamb.

Feeding him all sorts of unsuitable food. Mints, bars of chocolate. Letting him lie all day in front of the television. No wonder he bit people. Bored, wretched creature. And now abandoned, cast aside like a worn-out glove. It was no thanks to Mary that the wolves weren't tearing him to shreds that minute.

William bent to lift the cushion from its nest on the damp grass. There was mud on one corner, and streaks of cobwebs from the shed. He was reaching out a hand when two things happened.

First, Mary screamed. Second, a wolf leapt from behind the compost heap. It might have been the other way round: the wolf and then the scream. William never sorted it out properly. Whatever way, the combined effect was to send William up the path to the house like a rocket.

His mother moved even faster. She had been in the kitchen when William went out. Now he could see her crouching beside the sofa with her arms round Mary.

'What's going on?' she said crossly when William made a dramatic entrance through the patio window as if all the hounds of hell were chasing him. 'If this is more silly make-believe . . .'

'I didn't do anything,' William shouted. 'Ask her. I wasn't here, was I? I was outside, fetching the blue –' He broke off. He hadn't fetched it, he realized. His hands were empty.

Mary lifted a tearful face. 'William!' she sobbed brokenly. 'The wolves got William!'

'No they didn't.' William was puzzled, and rather touched. He hadn't thought she cared so much. 'I'm here. I'm all right. Look.'

'Not you – Lamb! Lamb was William!' With another wail, Mary flung herself face down on the sofa.

William – Lamb? William turned the words round in his mind, trying to make sense of them.

'I hope you're satisfied,' said his mother fiercely. 'I told you how it would be.' William had no answer. He was too stunned to speak.

Lamb – William? Mary had called Lamb after him? William leant his head against the glass. He felt very tired. The blue cushion lay on the grass where he'd

left it. The wolves were gone.

Behind him Mary was still crying – crying for Lamb, William realized. She loved him. She loved . . . William.

William went over to the sofa. 'It's all right, Mary. Lamb's all right. The wolves didn't get him.'

'They did. I saw them. That's why I screamed. And then they ate him. They ate Lamb.' The tears trickled down Mary's cheeks and fell on to the sofa. 'They ate WILLIAM!'

'They didn't,' William said again. 'I was there, remember? I saw what happened. A –' he swallowed hard: what he was about to say went against all his principles '– a chimpanzee saved him. It swung down and picked Lamb up just as the wolf was coming. It carried him up on to the roof of the shed.'

'Then what?' Mary sniffed hopefully. 'Then what happened?'

'Then they had a tea-party,' said William woodenly. 'All the chimpanzees and Lamb together.'

'With the yellow tea-set?'

'With the yellow tea-set.' William braced himself for the insult that was coming.

'That's my best one.' Mary took a handkerchief from her mother and blew her nose in a business-like way. Her mother went back to the kitchen. 'Will they have another tea-party tomorrow?'

'No,' said William. Enough was enough. 'The chimpanzees said goodbye and went back to Africa. That's where they came from. And the wolves went back to Siberia –' Suddenly he saw them, small and far away, slinking along a track beneath tall trees. On the crest of a hill, they halted and looked back. Then, without haste, they made their way down the slope and out of sight.

'And the snakes?'

'The snakes went back to . . .' William's imagination was wearing thin.

'Back to Mrs Evans's garden,' said Mary comfortably. 'I'll go and get Lamb now.' At the window she hesitated. 'You can share him if you want to, William.'

'No, that's all right,' said William hurriedly.

'It's more fun if you share things.'

'We'll share something else, then.' Saying goodbye to the wolves was one thing. Taking shares in Lamb was another. You have to draw the line somewhere.

'All right, William.'

William nodded approvingly. Mary wasn't so hard to deal with when you knew how. You had to be firm, that's all.

Next morning William awoke and stretched, feeling better than he had for a long time. The first thing he saw when he turned his head was the blue cushion beside his pillow.

William frowned. Mary needn't think he was going to keep it on his bed permanently. Alternate nights, that was how it was going to be from now on.

Still, while Lamb was there, he might as well make use of the horrible creature.

William bundled the cushion under one arm and reached for a book. Quite useful, a cushion that size, really. He might let Mary leave it there after all.

William settled himself comfortably on the bed and read on.